TREE-HOUSE COMIX Proudly Presents

CAT KID
COMIC CLUB

WRITTEN AND ILLUSTRATED BY **DAV PILKEY**

AS GEORGE BEARD AND HAROLD HUTCHINS

WITH COLOR BY JOSE GARIBALDI

SQUID KID AND KATYDID

An EPiC Sneak Preview by Molly and Li'l Petey

graphix

AN IMPRINT OF

SCHOLASTIC

TO CLAIR FREDERICK AND THE MERRYMAKERS, INC. TEAM

Library of Congress Control Number 2020938611

978-1-338-71276-6 (POB)
978-1-338-71277-3 (Library)

10 9 8 7 6 5 4 3 2 1   20 21 22 23 24

Printed in China   62
First edition, December 2020

Edited by Ken Geist
Lettering and art by Dav Pilkey
Book design by Dav Pilkey and Phil Falco
Color by Jose Garibaldi
Color flatting by Aaron Polk
Publisher: David Saylor

CHAPTERS & COMICS

((23))

Hey, guys...

...Welcome to the **FiRST** meeting of...

...The CAT KiD COMiC CLUB!!!

HOORAY!!!

11

... and draw a line on your paper...

... like this.

Now on the **LEFT** side, write **Five** things you **Love.**

Pizza
BubbleGum
Squids
Videos
Katydid

Comics
Fireflies
Popcorn
Frien

Okay. Now on the other side...

...write five things ya like to **DO!!!**

Play
read
Laugh
Write
Draw

Actually, that's Pretty Good!!!

Now let's all try to think up an idea...

...by using stuff from Melvin's lists!

PLAY
read
Laugh
write
DRaw

He could write about a Dinosaur who likes to brush his teeth.

OR a nerd who likes to Annoy people.

Dennis the Toothbrush Who Wanted to be a Dinosaur Lawyer

By: Melvin the Frog

One time there was a
toothbrush...

... named Dennis...

... who wanted to be a
Lawyer.

For Dinosaurs.

So...

.. Yeah.

The END.

About the Author

Melvin the Frog

No Bell
Peace
Prize For
Graphic Novels

Caldebery Award

Melvin the Frog is widely known as one of the world's most important Major voices in Graphic Literature.

He has won ~~the too~~ countless Awards for his Genius and awesome humility. His awesomeness has inspired countless ~~Ge~~ Generations and stuff.

COMING SOON:

Dennis the toothbrush Who wanted to be a Dinosaur Lawyer 2: Cretaceous Court

Well, that was dumb.

HEY!

WE DO **NOT TALK** TO EACH OTHER LIKE THAT, NAOMI!

But I WAS just being **HONEST!**

DO YOU NEED TO GO SIT ON THE TIME-OUT ROCK?

NO.

Hey, guys. Welcome to day 2 of the Cat Kid Com—

Excuse me, Molly.

Before you begin, Naomi has something she'd like to say.

Naomi?

Um... well... I...

I'm sorry I said your comic was dumb, Melvin.

Did **ANYBODY** work on their comic last night?

I couldn't think of any good ideas.

Me neither.

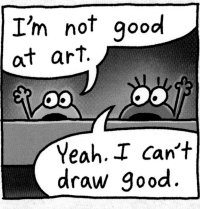

I'm not good at art.

Yeah. I can't draw good.

So **NOBODY** made a comic Last night???

I tried, but it was dumb.

I ripped mine up.

I can't spell good.

What **IS** your **Thing?**

Summer likes photography.

And Starla is a **POET!**

Oh.

Well comics don't have to be **STORIES!**

They could be **POEMS!**

CHAPTER 3

FOUR FABULOUS FLOPS

MonsTer CHeese sandwich

★ Story by: Naomi ★ Art by: Corky
★ coLor by: Pink ★ Lettering by:
kendrick

Momma had a little baby.

Little Baby was very hungry.

Gimme some food, man!

Ok

I will make a muenster cheese sandwich for you

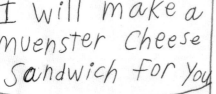

So she went to the fridge.

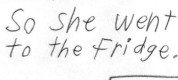

But Momma grabbed the wrong cheese by accident.

Momma cut the cheese.

chop

46

47

HOW 2 DRAW the Monster CHEESE SAndwich

in 17 Ridiculously easy steps

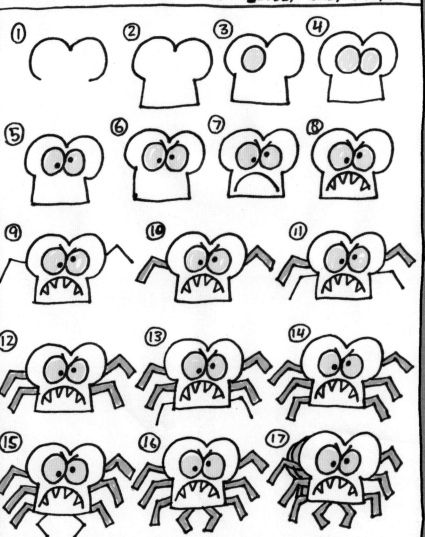

Author's Notes:

Naomi
the
Great

"This story is based on the truth. One time Daddy said he was going to make us Muenster cheese sandwiches, but I thought he said 'Monster cheese sandwiches.' I got scared and cried (I was really little). Now we all call muenster cheese 'Monster cheese' because we think it's funny but it wasn't at first." — Naomi the Great

About the Illustrator:

Corky

Corky has been an artist ever since he was a tadpole. His secret is to draw every day and don't give up even if you make lots of mistakes.

About the Colorist:

Pink

Pink loves music. He can play the ukulele pretty good. He also loves to sing and wrestle.

About the Letterer:

Kendrick

Kendrick the frog is an awesome dude. ~~when~~ He likes swimming and collecting stickers. When he is big, he will stay up as late as he wants.

MY DOG

by Pedro

MY DOG is BiG

MY DOG is AWEsome.

I Can have a DOG.

MY DOG Poops BiG Poops.

I DON'T Clean it up.

But then some Bad Ninja Guys attack.

55

MY DOG Saved the World.

The END.

About the Author and Illustrator

Pedro
Pedro is nice.
P.S. This story wasn't true. It is Fake. Pedro really doesn't have a dog but he wants one but Daddy says no every time but maybe I will some day when I am responsible.

The End.

How 2 Draw

MY DOG

in 14 ridonkulously easy steps.

57

HOW 2 DRAW MY DOG'S POOPs

in 3 ridonculously easy steps

① ② ③ now Give my DOG's Poops some personality!

eyes

smile

happy

sad

sleepy

Robot Poop

Bad guy Poop

Baby Poop

Lady Poop

Ninja Poop

Pirate Poop

mummy Poop

cyclops Poop

Betty Poop

winnie the Poop

spider Poop

Bat poop

Poobacca

Boba Poop

storm-pooper

58

SUPA FAiL

By K.T., Kip, and Curly

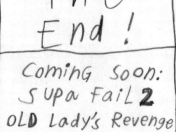

Meet the creators:

K.T. likes to Hang out with her brothers.

Kip Likes computers and Quesadillas

Curly Likes Pizza and Frosting.

I Thought You SAid YoUR Comic WASN'T OFFENSIVE!

It wasn't.

The Whole WoRLD GoT DESTRoYed!

Billions of PeoPLe Died!

oh Yeah.

ALL because of A TooThPicK?

I'm VERY **Disturbed** by these comics!!!

They're Just So **AWFUL!**

I thought they were **SUPPOSED** to be awful!!!

How about you, Poppy?

I'll bet **YOU** made Something **NICE!**

I did, Daddy!!! It's called "The Cute, Little, Fluffy Cloud...

... of Death."

72

The Cute, Little, Fluffy Cloud of Death

by Poppy

Once there was a cute, little cloud.

She was fluffy and dead.

Hi   Hi

But the sun was mean to her.

HEY

You're creeping me out!!!

GO AWAY

So the cute, little, fluffy cloud of death cried and cried

The End

about the author

 Poppy is a Frog who Lives with her Family in a Camper by the Pond. She Likes Ghosts and skeletons and drawing and monsters and rain. She ~~likes~~ likes to draw every day because it is Fun. ALso, she likes Dogs.

the end.

Let's make a comic About **POOP WARS!**

And we got an idea about **Evil Zombies!**

I'm gonna make a story about a **DEAD AIRPLANE!**

I'll use felt, glue, and construction paper!

And I'm gonna make **DENNIS The TOOTHBRUSH: DINOSAUR LAWYER 2!**

CHAPTER 4
NEW RULES

From now on, everyone's comics must be **WHOLESOME...**

...and **UpLiFTiNG...**

...with **GOOD VALueS** and **MORALS!!!**

Before you kids start your comic club today...

...I want to apologize.

I'm sorry if I discouraged you yesterday.

I shouldn't have let **MY TASTES** spoil everything.

You kids should write stories that make **YOU** happy.

Write things that make **YOU** laugh!

Dennis the Toothbrush who Wanted to be a DINOSAUR Lawyer 2: Cretaceous Courtroom

JUDGE

By Melvin

FUN FACTS about the cast

SPINOSAURUSES

Lived on Land and water. Their fins may have been used to heat up their body Quickly, or to Attract a mate.

Length: over 50 Feet ★ Weight: over 6 Tons ★ carnivore ★ Cretaceous Period

Triceratopses

were vegetarians that had 800 teeth. Their Worst enemy was the T. Rex.

Length: up To 30 Feet ★ Weight: up to 13 Tons ★ Cretaceous Period

IGuanoDons

had Five Fingers and could ~~grasp~~ grasp things with their hands. Their Thumbs had big spikes on them. sweeeet!!!

Size: up to 43 Feet Long ★ Weight: over 8 Tons ★ vegan ★ Cretaceous Period

Toothbrushes were invented in 1977 by Dr. William Brush. He named them after his daughter, "Toothetta". They are mainly used For oral hygiene and are not Known to practice Law.

Size: up to 10 inches ★ Weight: 6 Ounces ★ Diet: PLAQUE ★ Disco ERA To present

About the Genius Worker:

Coolest Author Award of All-Time. NO Takebacks

Toothetta Brush Memorial Award.

Peel it, sir Prize For Literature

Melvin the Frog is the multiple major award-winning author and illustrator of over 1 Graphic novels.

Known throughout the globe for his intelligence and Dashing good Looks, Melvin is also regarded as a Key influencer and a trend-setting fashion guru.

How can one Frog be so Awesome? Scientists are Working around the clock to solve this mystery.

"The world may never know," said the world's Second-Smartest person, Dr. Gene Yiss.

Fans and admirers of Melvin can purchase his autograph For $1.00 While supplies Last. Buy Ten, get the <u>eleventh</u> For 1/2 Price!!!

Very Good, Melvin!

Yeah! That was **WAY BETTER** than last time!

I told him to put Dinosaurs in it!!!

I WAS GOING TO ANYWAY!

And I'm not tryin' to **TATTLE** or anything, but...

I saw him **COPYING** how to draw out of a **BOOK!!!**

BIRDS
FLOWERS
TREES

HAIKU AND
PHOTOS BY
SUMMER
AND
STARLA

Little flower buds
Even if no one can see
Open anyway

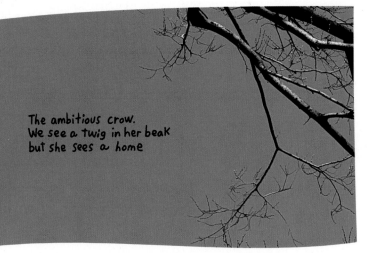

The ambitious crow.
We see a twig in her beak
but she sees a home

From a great distance
branches pierce the sapphire sky
like dark lightning bolts

but branches up close
will tell another story:
one of potential

If you look closely
you can find marvelous things
that yearn to be seen.

If you look closer
you might find something hidden
deep in the shadows.

Which of these are we?
Shall we hide or brightly shine?
We cannot do both

We are very small

but the things inside our hearts

Could fill up the sky

About Haiku
by Summer & Starla

haiku are poems
with seventeen syllables
they come from Japan

the syllables are
divided into three lines
five, seven, and five

they tell stories of
nature and beauty and truth
simple and profound

even though haiku
may take decades to master
kids write the best ones

About the poet and the photo-grapher:

Summer and Starla
are artists and BFFs
but they're sisters, first

Starla loves to read
to disappear in a book
to get lost in words

Summer dreams about
dinosaurs and string theory
she also loves crêpes

CHAPTER 8

The Show and Tell Party

The next day...

Well, we've come to the end of our **First week!**

So Let's PARTY!

PARTY Time

YAY! YAY!

HOORAY!!!

I made Monster Cheese sandwiches for everybody!!!

And I can draw faces on them if you want!!!

SQUID KID AND KATYDID

An epic Sneak Preview by Molly and Li'l Petey

Baby Flippy

A Sneak Peek by
Wendy and Raine

Wendy and Raine proudly present:

A True Story of Courage.

Baby Flippy

Before he was Daddy...

...he was *DINNER!*

COMING SOON

to a Cat Kid Comic Club near you!

Wait a minute...

...I don't remember buying you these action figures!

You didn't.

We modified all of our broken figures...

...Using putty, glue, pipe cleaners, and paint...

...To create **ALL-NEW** Heroes and villains!!!

CHUBBS McSPIDERBUTT

An Epic Preview by The HACKER Bros.

...and the butt of a spider!

CHUBBS McSPiDERBUTT

An Epic Photo-Comic by The H.A.C.K.E.R. BRothers
(Heroic Alpha Commando Kids: Elite Regiment)

STARRiNG

Zeus Goldberg as CHubbs McSpiderbutt

Wei Chan as Jake the Flying Spider

Brock Manhammer as Dr. Pasty McSprinkles

And Introducing Scott the Worm as Scott the Worm

COMING SOON

That was very good, boys...

...but I don't understand...

...How did all of your action figures get broken?

Oh. Because we threw 'em off the—

They broke all by themselves by accident.

Alright, would anyone else like to share their Preview?

We would, Daddy!

We're making a comic with clay and cardboard and stuff!

I wrote the story...

...And we made the art!

BABY FROG
SQUAD

Story By: Billie

Art by: Frida, EL, and Deb

Once upon a time...

...there were three baby frogs...

...who went to the Police Academy.

They studied hard...

... learned Kung-fu...

... and directed lots of traffic!

But soon, they got tired of working for the Man!

Soon, a bully was detected on planet #39.

Let's Go!

And so...

RAAAR!!!

HeY! Quit bullying that little dude!!!

MAKE Me!!!

I don't make cupcakes!

I eat 'em for BREAKFAST!

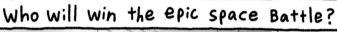

Who will win the epic space Battle?

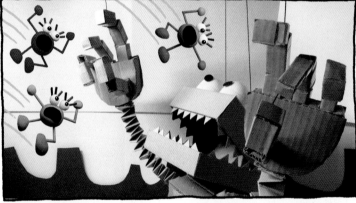

Find out in...

BABY FROG SQUAD

COMING SOON!

I thought you were trying to be more chill, Daddy.

Do you need to sit on the time-out rock?

I—I'm sorry I yelled at you, kids.

Don't worry, Daddy!

It's just like we learned this week:

NOTES & FUN FACTS

✮ Chubbs McSpiderbutt was made from a broken action figure, epoxy putty, enamel paint, and 48 black pipe cleaners (chenille stems) twisted together to make his legs.

✮ The robot bully in BABY FROG SQUAD was made out of cardboard, hot glue, tape, paper clips, and plastic salad dressing lids (for the eyeballs).

✮ The baby frogs in BABY FROG SQUAD were made with Japanese rice clay (eyes, bodies, hands, and feet) and toothpicks painted with acrylics and markers (limbs and eyelashes).

✮ The pencils on page 164 are toothpicks colored with markers.

✮ Summer and Starla's poetic description of haiku on page 125 is NOT definitive. The art of haiku is ever-evolving and has a rich, complex history. English-language haiku first appeared in the late 19th century. They were based on Japanese poems called renga, which were structured, improvised verse poetry collaborations, often performed live. The first stanza of a renga, called the hokku, became what we commonly think of as haiku.

✮ One of the oldest and most famous Japanese haiku (technically a hokku) has a frog in it.

> Breaking the silence
> Of an ancient pond,
> A frog jumped into the water—
> A deep resonance.

> —Bashō (1644-1694)
> Translated by
> Nobuyuki Yuasa

GET READING
WITH DAV PILKEY!

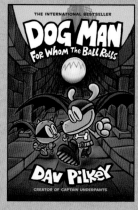

ABOUT THE
AUTHOR-ILLUSTRATOR

When Dav Pilkey was a kid, he was diagnosed with ADHD and dyslexia. Dav was so disruptive in class that his teachers made him sit out in the hallway every day. Luckily, Dav loved to draw and make up stories. He spent his time in the hallway creating his own original comic books — the very first adventures of Dog Man and Captain Underpants.

In college, Dav met a teacher who encouraged him to illustrate and write. He won a national competition in 1986 and the prize was the publication of his first book, WORLD WAR WON. He made many other books before being awarded the 1998 California Young Reader Medal for DOG BREATH, which was published in 1994, and in 1997 he won the Caldecott Honor for THE PAPERBOY.

THE ADVENTURES OF SUPER DIAPER BABY, published in 2002, was the first complete graphic novel spin-off from the Captain Underpants series and appeared at #6 on the USA Today bestseller list for all books, both adult and children's, and was also a New York Times bestseller. It was followed by THE ADVENTURES OF OOK AND GLUK: KUNG FU CAVEMEN FROM THE FUTURE and SUPER DIAPER BABY 2: THE INVASION OF THE POTTY SNATCHERS, both USA Today bestsellers. The unconventional style of these graphic novels is intended to encourage uninhibited creativity in kids.

His stories are semi-autobiographical and explore universal themes that celebrate friendship, tolerance, and the triumph of the good-hearted.

Dav loves to kayak in the Pacific Northwest with his wife.